"Dad loves the strawberry jam his mom used to make, right? So we'll make some for him. He'll love it!" Bradley pointed at the ripe strawberries in the garden. "And we'll use our own berries!"

"We don't know how to make jam," Brian said.

"How hard can it be?" asked Bradley. "Besides, I know Dad kept his mom's recipes in a box. There might be one for jam."

"Forget about making jam from these strawberries," Lucy said. "Something is eating them. Look at this one—it's bitten in half."

"This one is, too," Nate said. "And that one! Something is biting all the berries!"

endar MYSTeries

June
Jam

GRANDMA'S JAM

by Ron Roy

**illustrated by
John Steven Gurney**

A STEPPING STONE BOOK™

Random House 🏠 New York

Dedicated to Chris
—**R.R.**

To Mark and Julia
—**J.S.G.**

This is a work of fiction. Names, characters, places, and incidents either are the product of the author's imagination or are used fictitiously. Any resemblance to actual persons, living or dead, events, or locales is entirely coincidental.

Text copyright © 2011 by Ron Roy
Cover art and interior illustrations copyright © 2011 by John Steven Gurney

Published in the United States by Random House Children's Books,
a division of Random House, Inc., New York.

Random House and the colophon are registered trademarks and A Stepping Stone Book and the colophon are trademarks of Random House, Inc.

Visit us on the Web!
SteppingStonesBooks.com
ronroy.com
www.randomhouse.com/kids

Educators and librarians, for a variety of teaching tools, visit us at
www.randomhouse.com/teachers

Library of Congress Cataloging-in-Publication Data
Roy, Ron.
June jam / by Ron Roy ; illustrated by John Steven Gurney.
    p.   cm. — (Calendar mysteries)
"A Stepping Stone book."
Summary: As a Father's Day gift to the twins' dad, Bradley, Brian, and their friends
Lucy and Nate try to identify and stop whatever creature is biting fruits and vegetables
in the garden.
ISBN 978-0-375-86112-3 (trade) — ISBN 978-0-375-96112-0 (lib. bdg.) —
ISBN 978-0-375-89833-4 (ebook)
[1. Mystery and detective stories. 2. Gardens—Fiction. 3. Pests—Fiction.
4. Father's Day—Fiction. 5. Twins—Fiction. 6. Brothers and sisters—Fiction.
7. Cousins—Fiction.] I. Gurney, John Steven, ill. II. Title.
PZ7.R8139Jun 2011
[Fic]—dc22
2010028382

Printed in the United States of America

10 9 8 7

Contents

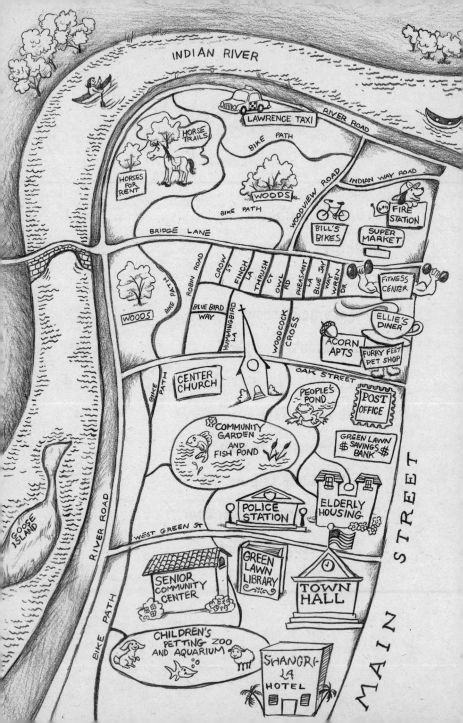

WELCOME TO

GREEN LAWN

HOME OF THE

Calendar **Mysteries**

N
W — E
S

BOAT LAUNCH

RIVER ROAD

BOAT RENTAL

RON'S BAIT

DUCK WALK WAY

GREEN LAWN MIDDLE SCHOOL

FARM LANE

EAGLE LANE

BRADLEY + BRIAN

MEADOW ROAD

GREEN LAWN ELEMENTARY SCHOOL

LUCY

NATE

TREE TO CIRCLE

FOX LANE

QUAIL RUN ROAD

SILVER CIRCLE

WOODY STREET

BAND SHELL

ROSE GARDEN

PLEASANT STREET

THISTLE COURT

WILDFLOWER WAY

CENTER PARK

ROSE STREET

SWAN POND

GREEN LAWN HIGH SCHOOL

PLAYING FIELDS

GYM + POOL

BOXWOOD LANE

HOWARD'S BARBER SHOP

BOOK NOOK

GAS STATION

CRYSTAL POND

MYSTIC GREENHOUSE

DOG KENNEL VETERINARIAN

RIVER ROAD

EAST GREEN STREET

TOWN TENNIS COURTS

TOWN SWIMMING POOL

KIDDIE POOL

TOWN BASEBALL FIELD

TO THE BLUE HILLS

1
Saturday Chores

Bradley Pinto and his twin brother, Brian, climbed into the backseat of the family car. Their older brother, Josh, got in front next to their dad.

"How come you always get to sit up front?" Brian asked.

"Because I'm older and wiser," Josh said.

Their father smiled.

"Dad, thanks for taking us out for breakfast," Bradley said.

"You're welcome, Bradley," his father answered. "Did you three get enough to eat?"

"I sure did!" Josh said. "I'll never eat again."

"Yeah, right," Brian said. "For at least an hour."

Bradley picked up the *Junior Encyclopedia* he'd been reading in the car. His teacher had asked each student to study one encyclopedia volume. Each kid had drawn a letter out of a bag. Bradley had gotten the letter *J*. So far, he had read about jaguars, Japanese fishing villages, javelin throwing, juggling, jungles, and a bunch of other stuff. He looked at a page about jam.

"Why do you always have strawberry jam on your toast?" Bradley asked.

His father grinned. "What else is there?"

"Butter, marshmallow spread, peanut butter, grape jelly, lots of stuff!" Brian said.

"Your grandmother Pinto, my mom,

used to make strawberry jam when I was a kid," their father said. "I had her jam sandwiches for a snack every day after school. Her jam was the best in the world. Now that she's gone, I keep trying to find strawberry jam that tastes as good as hers. So far, I haven't found it."

The car pulled into their driveway. "Don't forget your Saturday chores," Bradley's father said.

"Aw, Dad, I was gonna play softball," Josh said.

"Okay, but after you clean the barn," his father said. "If you get cracking, you'll be done in an hour."

"What's our job?" Bradley asked.

"You two can weed the garden," his father said.

"Do we get paid?" Brian asked.

His father laughed. "Yes! You get to sleep in a bed, and you get to have three meals a day!"

They all climbed out of the car. "Change your clothes first," the boys' father said.

"Can Lucy and Nate come over and help?" Bradley asked.

"Sure, if they want to," his father said.

"Okay, then I'm getting Dink and Ruth Rose to help me in the barn," Josh announced.

"Fine," his father said. "Tell you what—if you kids do a great job, I'll buy ice cream later for everyone."

The three boys tore up the stairs to their bedrooms. While Bradley and Brian were changing their clothes, their mother knocked and poked her head into the room. "How was breakfast?" she asked.

"Awesome, Mom," Bradley said.

"Why didn't you come, too?" Brian asked.

"I wanted to stay home to think about a present for Daddy," their mom said.

"Why, is it his birthday?" Bradley asked.

She shook her head. "No, Father's Day is tomorrow."

After she left, the twins finished changing. "I'll call Lucy and Nate," Bradley said.

"See you downstairs," Brian said.

Bradley called Lucy Armstrong. She was visiting her cousin Dink while her parents were in Arizona helping to build a school. Dink lived next door to Nate and Ruth Rose. Bradley, Brian, Lucy, and Nate were best friends.

Josh, Dink, and Ruth Rose were all twelve and had been friends since kindergarten.

Bradley ran out to the garden. "They're coming," he told his brother.

"Good," Brian said. He pointed at the ground. "It'll only take a million years to pull all these weeds."

"No, it won't," Bradley said. "We can divide it up in sections. You take the tomatoes, Nate can do the lettuce, and Lucy will do around the zucchini."

"What part will you do?" Brian asked.

"I'll weed around the strawberries," Bradley said. "Hey, there they are!"

Lucy and Nate walked into the garden through the gate.

"Thanks for coming over to help, guys," Bradley said.

"I think weeding is fun," Lucy told him. "I weed our garden in California all the time."

"I hate weeding," Nate said.

"My dad is buying us ice cream when we finish," Brian told Nate.

"I love weeding!" Nate said.

They all laughed.

"Let's start," Bradley said. He told the other kids their sections.

All four kids got down on their knees and started pulling weeds. They threw them into a pile in the corner of the garden. The sun warmed their backs.

"How much ice cream do we get?" Nate asked.

"Ten gallons each!" Brian said.

"Brian, I just thought of what we can get Dad for Father's Day," Bradley said. "We'll make him some strawberry jam!"

Brian looked at his twin brother. "Jam?"

"Not just any jam," Bradley explained. "Dad loves the strawberry jam his mom used to make, right? So we'll make some for him. He'll love it!"

Bradley pointed at the ripe strawberries in the garden. "And we'll use our own berries!"

"We don't know how to make jam," Brian said.

"How hard can it be?" asked Bradley. "Besides, I know Dad kept his mom's recipes in a box. There might be one for jam."

"Forget about making jam from these strawberries," Lucy said. "Something is eating them. Look at this one—it's bitten in half."

"This one is, too," Nate said. "And that one! Something is biting all the berries!"

The kids got down on their knees. They checked all the strawberry plants.

"They're all bitten!" Brian said.

"This is horrible!" Bradley said.

"There's a strawberry monster in our garden!" Brian yelled.

2
Garden Monster

Bradley flopped down on the ground. "Nearly every berry is bitten in half!" he cried. "There aren't enough good ones left to make jam!"

"You could make zucchini jam," Nate suggested.

"Funny, Nate," Brian said.

Lucy looked at some of the zucchini. "Guys, it's not just the strawberries," she said. "Something is chewing on the vegetables, too. See, the same kind of bites."

"Oh no!" Brian said. "Dad is gonna freak when he finds out!"

"You'd better find whatever critter is doing this," Lucy said. "Otherwise, it will eat everything!"

Nate looked around nervously. "What if it's a snake?"

"Maybe it's birds," Brian said. "They could fly right in!"

Lucy picked up one of the bitten strawberries. "No, this doesn't look like a bird bite," she said. "Or a rabbit or a snake."

"What kind of bite does it look like?" Bradley asked.

Lucy turned the berry over and showed the boys. "It's a big, round bite," she said. "I think I've seen bites like this before."

She looked at the boys. "In the desert near where we live, there are lizards called Gila monsters. They eat birds' eggs and small animals, but sometimes they come into people's gardens," she said. "And they're poisonous."

"Great, we've got a poisonous monster in our garden!" Brian said.

Lucy laughed. "No, you don't," she said. "Gila monsters only live in hot, dry places. They'd die in Connecticut because it gets too cold here. But we once had one in our garden, and the bite is the same. They make just one chomp, with no chewing or nibbling."

"I'm not staying here to weed," Nate cried. "I want to keep all ten toes!"

"What about the ice cream?" Brian asked.

"I don't need any ice cream!" Nate said.

Bradley laughed. "Yes, you do," he said.

"I just thought of what we can give Dad for Father's Day," Brian said.

"What?" Bradley asked.

"Well, since we can't make the jam because something's eating the berries, we can find whatever is doing it," Brian said. "We'll save Dad's garden, and that will be his present!"

Bradley kicked a stone. "I still want to make the jam," he muttered. "Did you see Dad's face when he told us about Grandma Pinto's jam that he used to eat?"

"We still have to catch whatever is biting all this stuff," Lucy said.

"What if it's a skunk?" Brian asked. He was grinning.

"Or a monkey!" Nate said.

"It could be a slug," Brian said.

"EEEEWWWWW!" Nate yelled. "I'm not touching any slug!"

"Guys, get serious," Bradley said. He looked at the fence his father had built around the garden. "Whatever is eating

the stuff climbed over that!"

Nate stood next to the fence and held his hand up. "This fence is three feet tall," he said. "No little animal could get over it."

"Something might have dug under

the fence," Lucy said. "Let's look for holes."

The kids checked every inch of the ground under the fence, all around the garden.

"Nothing crawled under," Bradley said.

The four kids looked at each other.

"Well, if it can't get over the fence," Nate said, "and it didn't go under the fence, it must have gone right through the fence!"

"It's a ghost!" Brian said.

Bradley laughed at his brother. "I don't think ghosts eat strawberries. But Lucy's right. We have to catch whatever it is," he said. "Otherwise Dad won't have a garden, let alone strawberries."

3

Lucy's Great Idea

"How do we catch something we can't see?" Nate asked.

Bradley thought about what he'd been reading in the encyclopedia about jungles. He remembered a section that showed people catching animals.

"I have some ideas," he said. "But first, let's finish weeding the garden."

"If I see one thing with legs and a mouth, I'm out of here!" Nate said.

"We all have legs and mouths," Brian teased.

Nate giggled. "You know what I mean," he said.

The four kids got busy. They yanked every weed they could find and threw them in the pile. Bradley removed every strawberry that had been bitten. There were some ripe red ones left, and a lot that would turn red soon.

The kids were hot, dirty, and sweaty when they finished. The boys took off their T-shirts and hung them on the fence. Then they sprayed each other with the garden hose.

"I just had an idea," Lucy said. She pointed at the three T-shirts on the fence. "We could build a scarecrow and stand it in the garden. It might scare the mystery creature into staying away."

"How do you make a scarecrow?" asked Brian.

"It's easy," Lucy said. "I helped my folks build one back home. We need wood, nails, and some old clothes to dress it in."

"There's wood and nails in the barn," Brian said.

"I could get some of my dad's old clothes," Bradley said.

"Why can't we use our own?" Brian asked.

"Too small," Lucy said. "You want big, floppy shirts and pants."

"Cool," Bradley said. "We'll meet in the barn after I talk to my father."

The boys put their shirts back on.

Brian, Nate, and Lucy ran into the barn. Bradley cut across the yard.

"Dad, I need your clothes!" he yelled as he entered the kitchen.

Bradley's father was standing at the stove. He was humming and stirring something in a pot. The kitchen smelled like tomato sauce. Pal, the family's basset hound, was under the table, snoring.

"My clothes?" he asked. "You want me to cook in my underwear?"

Bradley laughed. "Not what you're wearing now," he said. "Old clothes."

"Why do you want my old clothes?" his father asked.

"Um, it's a surprise!" Bradley said.

"Well, okay. Go ask your mom. I think she's upstairs."

"Thanks, Dad." Bradley ran up the stairs. His parents' bedroom door was closed. He knocked. "Mom? Are you awake?"

"Come in," his mother called.

She was reading, but put down her book and smiled. "Why is your hair wet, Bradley?"

"We're weeding the garden and I got hot," he said. Bradley told his mother about the creature that was eating the strawberries and vegetables. He left out the part about wanting to make jam for Father's Day. He still wanted to do it, but he wanted it to be a surprise. "We want to make a scarecrow," he said.

"What a good idea!" his mother said. She got up off the bed and opened the door to their big closet. "Okay, here's a shirt I've been wanting to throw out for a year!" She handed Bradley an old blue flannel shirt. "And take these jeans.

They have paint stains all over the knees."

Bradley's mother winked. "Don't tell Daddy," she whispered.

4
Scary Scarecrow

Bradley carried the shirt and jeans across the yard to the barn. Josh, Dink, and Ruth Rose were sweeping the floor. They had piled a lot of stuff on the workbench. Bradley noticed a tricycle he used to ride. He also saw an old basketball and a rolled-up fishing net.

At the other end of the barn, Brian, Nate, and Lucy were looking through a pile of boards.

"Mom let me have Dad's old shirt and jeans," he told the other kids.

"They'll be perfect," Lucy said.

"So what do we do?" Brian asked. "I got a hammer and nails."

Lucy pulled out some thin boards. "This tall one can be the body," she said. "And these can be the arms and legs. We just nail them together."

"That's supposed to scare animals away?" Nate said. "It'll just be a big stick figure."

"No, it'll look like a big human after we put the shirt and pants on and stuff it with straw," Lucy explained.

The kids knelt on the floor. Lucy arranged the boards. "See? Arms and legs. Who wants to hammer?" she asked.

"I will," Nate said.

Brian handed Nate a nail. "Don't hit your thumb," he said.

"I won't," Nate said. He held the nail in place, lifted the hammer, and hit his thumb.

"Ouch!" he said.

"Told you," Brian said.

"Let me try," Bradley said, taking the hammer. "I helped my dad build a bird-house last year."

Soon the boards were nailed together.

"Okay, now we dress him," Lucy said.

The kids tugged the shirt and jeans onto the wood frame.

"He looks like he's starving," Nate said.

"Grab some straw," Lucy said. "We'll make him look fat!"

They each brought an armful of straw and began filling the shirt and jeans.

"Give him a big chest," Brian said. "He'll look like a giant!"

Bradley found some rope, and they tied it around the scarecrow's waist for a belt. They tied more around his wrists and ankles so the straw wouldn't fall out. When they were done, the scarecrow looked almost real.

"He's cool!" Nate said. "Except for one thing. He needs a head."

"Wait a sec," Bradley said. He ran into Polly's stall. His pony was munching from her pail of oats. He patted her neck, then took the empty oats bag. It said OATS on one side, but the bag would make a perfect scarecrow head.

He ran back to the others. "How's this?" he asked.

"Great," Lucy said. "Stuff it with straw."

After the head was filled with straw, the kids tied it onto the frame with more rope.

"It's not very scary," Brian said. "But I know how to fix that!" He raced out of the barn toward the house.

"We could draw a scary face with Magic Markers," Bradley suggested.

"Let's splash his face with red paint that looks like blood!" Nate said.

Brian ran back into the barn. He showed the other kids a Halloween mask. The face had warts, snaggly teeth, a big scar, and one eyeball hanging out of its socket.

"What do you think?" Brian asked.

"Awesome!" Nate said.

Bradley laughed. "Cool, Brian. Not even Dad will go in the garden when he sees this!"

Brian tugged the mask over the stuffed oats bag.

"Okay, let's bring him outside," Lucy said.

The kids each took an arm or a leg, and they lugged the scarecrow into the garden. Josh, Dink, and Ruth Rose stared as the younger kids and the scarecrow moved through the barn.

They used rope to tie the scarecrow to the fence.

"That is so amazingly awesome!" Nate said.

"It looks like someone I know," Brian said. He closed his eyes, pretending to think. "Oh yeah! It looks like you, Bradley."

Bradley grinned. "Well, if it looks like me, then it looks like you, twin brother!"

5
Grandma's Recipe

The kids stood back and admired their scarecrow.

"It would sure scare me if I was eating your garden!" Nate said.

"Me too," Lucy said. "The one we made in California looked a lot friendlier than this one does."

"I hope it keeps the mystery creature out of the garden," Bradley said.

"When do we get the ice cream?" Nate asked.

"Later," Bradley said. "But I'm really

thirsty. Let's go get a drink."

The kids trooped into the kitchen. The room smelled like spaghetti sauce. A pot was simmering on the stove. Pal was still asleep.

Brian took a pitcher of lemonade from the fridge. Bradley found some cookies. They sat around the kitchen table for their snack. Pal woke up and waited for cookie crumbs to fall.

"Maybe we could make Dad some cookies for Father's Day," Brian suggested as he munched. "He likes cookies."

Bradley shook his head. "He likes his mom's strawberry jam better," he said.

Bradley saw the recipe box on the counter. On top of the box was the recipe for Grandma Pinto's spaghetti sauce. He opened the box and flipped through the cards. "Here it is!" he said. He showed the card to the other kids as he read the directions out loud:

Strawberry Jam

1. Wash 1/2 pound of berries.
2. Mash berries.
3. Add one cup white sugar and one tablespoon lemon juice.
4. Stir over low heat until sugar dissolves.
5. Increase heat and boil for ten minutes.
6. Let cool before eating. Store in refrigerator.

"Uh-oh," Brian said. "We've got a problem."

"What problem?" Nate asked.

"We can't use the stove," Brian said.

"Why not?" Lucy asked.

"We're not allowed to cook without a grown-up," Bradley said.

"So what're we going to do?" asked Nate. "The recipe says to cook for ten minutes."

Bradley read the recipe again. "I say we leave that part out," he said. "We do everything else, but no cooking."

"That should be okay," Lucy said. "It's not like strawberries have to be cooked, right?"

Bradley slipped the card back into the box. "We probably won't be able to make it anyway," he said glumly. "Even if we do catch the mystery creature, we'll never get enough strawberries!"

"We could always give Dad an empty jar," Brian said. "We could put a note inside that says, WE REALLY WANTED TO MAKE YOU SOME JAM, BUT SOMETHING ATE ALL THE BERRIES."

Bradley tossed a cookie crumb at his brother. "Brilliant, Brian," he said. "Then when it's our birthday, Dad will give us an empty box with a note inside."

They all laughed.

Just then Josh, Dink, and Ruth Rose burst into the kitchen. They were dusty and sweaty from head to toe.

"I hope you left us some lemonade and cookies," Josh said.

"There's plenty left," Bradley said. The younger kids gave up their seats and walked outside.

"Look how the breeze makes the scarecrow seem like it's alive," Lucy said.

They walked over to the garden. Bradley went inside the fence. He bent down near the strawberry patch. Then he screamed.

"AHHHHH!"

6

Bradley's Monster Trap

"What's wrong?" Brian, Nate, and Lucy shouted. They all ran into the garden.

"LOOK!" Bradley said. He held up a strawberry. Something had taken a chunk out of it. "I know this one was perfect when we went in the house. I picked all the ones that had been bitten!"

"I guess the mystery creature was snacking on this while we were snacking on cookies," Brian said.

"Mr. Scarecrow isn't scary enough," Lucy said.

"What do we do now?" Nate asked.

"We get smart!" Bradley said. He ran into the house and came back with the *J* encyclopedia book. He turned to the jungle section and flipped pages.

"Um, what are you doing, bro?" Brian asked.

"We need to set a trap!" Bradley said. He showed them a picture of some people digging a hole in the ground. Another picture showed them covering the hole with branches and big leaves. A third picture showed a large animal falling into the hole while the people hid and watched. The last picture showed the people cooking the animal over a fire.

"We're gonna catch a water buffalo and eat him?" Nate asked.

"No, silly, we'll dig a smaller hole," Bradley said. "When we catch the creature, we'll take him out to the woods and let him go."

Lucy looked at the fence around the garden. "I still don't know how it got in here," she said.

"Maybe it's invisible!" Nate whispered. "He could be standing next to us right now, licking his lips! His fangs are long and shiny, his claws are sharp, and he's watching us!"

"And you're watching too much TV," Lucy said. "Bradley, we need a shovel."

"I'll get one," Brian said, and ran toward the barn door.

"Nate, can you find some thin branches or weeds to cover the hole?" Bradley asked.

"Back in a flash!" Nate said as he took off.

"Where should we dig the trap?" Brian asked when he returned with the shovel.

"Near the strawberries," Bradley said. "I'll dig first."

They all took turns digging in the soft garden soil. Soon the hole was round and deep.

Nate brought back a bunch of thin branches and weed stalks. The kids placed them across the hole carefully. Then Bradley sprinkled some garden mulch over the branches.

"It looks just like the rest of the ground," Lucy said.

"I wonder what we'll catch," Nate said.

"Whatever is eating the strawberries will never know there's a deep hole under there," Bradley said.

"Mom and Dad won't know there's a hole, either," Brian said. "If they step in it, they won't be very happy."

"You're right," Bradley said. "So we'll leave a note. Humans will know it's a trap, but . . ."

"THE MYSTERY CREATURE CAN'T READ!" the other kids yelled. They all did a quadruple high five in the garden.

Bradley wrote a note and left it on a stick next to the trap. The note said: DANGER! ANIMAL TRAP. DO NOT WALK HERE! He set a fat, ripe strawberry in the middle of the trap.

"Let's wait in the barn," Brian said.

The air in the barn was much cooler than outside in the sun. The floor was swept clean, and the workbench was neat. Bradley set his encyclopedia on the bench.

Polly the pony let out a loud whinny from her stall.

"She looks lonely," Lucy said. She ran over to pet the pony.

"And dirty!" Nate said. "Look at her coat!"

"It got real dusty in here when Josh and the guys were sweeping," Bradley said. "The dust blew all over poor Polly!"

"Let's wash her," Brian said. He went to the barn wall and turned on the spigot. Bradley picked up the hose and sprayed Polly's coat.

"There's some pony shampoo and brushes on the shelf," Brian told Nate and Lucy.

Soon Polly's coat was covered with

shampoo suds. The kids washed her
whole body, even her tail and mane and
hooves. Then Bradley rinsed her off.
"Let's take her out in the sun," he said.

Bradley led Polly out of the barn. She
shook her head, wetting them all with
water flying off her mane.

Brian brought a stack of old towels,
and the kids wiped Polly until her coat
gleamed.

While Bradley was drying Polly's

back legs, he glanced into the garden. He looked at his trap, but nothing seemed disturbed. Then he looked again.

"Oh no!" Bradley cried.

"What's wrong?" Lucy asked.

"The mystery creature struck again!" Bradley said.

7

The Long Neck

"What do you mean?" Nate asked. "The trap is just the way we left it. Nothing fell in, Bradley."

"It's not the way we left it," Bradley said. He opened the gate and ran into the garden. "I left a big strawberry right in the middle of it. Now look!"

He held up what was left of the strawberry. A bite had been taken out of it.

"I don't believe it!" Brian said. He moved the branches aside and peered down into the hole. "Nothing's down there."

"Something bit the berry without falling in!" Lucy said.

"It has to be some kind of bird," Nate announced. "It just flew in here, took a bite, then flew away again."

"I don't think so," Lucy said. "When birds peck at something, their beaks leave tiny holes." She pointed at the strawberry Bradley was holding. "See, half the berry is gone, but there are no beak holes. Some creature took a real bite!"

"Maybe it was something with a long neck," Brian said. "It could reach its neck out and take a bite without stepping on the trap!"

"Like what?" Bradley scoffed. "A giraffe?"

Nate laughed. "No, a python!"

"In Connecticut?" Brian asked.

Lucy giggled. "Maybe it was an octo-pus."

"They don't have necks," Bradley said.

"But they do have all those long arms!" Lucy answered. She waved her arms in the air.

Bradley threw the damaged straw-berry into the field behind the barn.

He kicked a rock into the fence.

"Now what do we do?" Nate asked again.

"Now we get mad!" Bradley said.

Just then Josh yelled from the house, "Lunch in five minutes, you guys! You too, Nate and Lucy!"

"Great, I'm starving!" Nate said.

"First we have to do something," Bradley said. "Come with me."

He ran into the barn and over to the workbench. "Help me get this down," he said.

"What?" Brian asked.

"Dad's seine," Bradley said.

"What's a seine?" Nate asked.

"A big fishing net," Bradley said. "It's that rolled-up thing."

The kids tugged the net off the bench. It plopped down on the barn floor.

"Our dad showed us how to catch minnows with this thing in the river," Brian said. "It's huge when it's opened."

The kids unrolled the net onto the floor. It was a big square, ten feet by ten feet.

"What're we going to do with it?" Nate asked.

"Cover the strawberries," Bradley said. "Come on, let's drag it outside."

The kids lugged the net through the door, through the gate, and into the garden.

"First, let's make sure there are no

more bitten berries," Bradley said.

They found a few that had been bitten and threw them into the field.

Then they each took a corner of the net and dropped it over the strawberry patch. Through the holes in the net, they could see several ripe strawberries.

"Something could still crawl under the net," Lucy said.

"Not when we're done," Bradley said. "Get those bricks."

There was a pile of bricks in the corner of the garden. The kids each grabbed some, and they laid them on the edges of the net, all around.

"Nothing is getting under there!" Brian said, wiping his hands on his shorts.

"I hope you're right," Bradley said. "Let's go eat!"

Bradley, Brian, Nate, and Lucy ran across the yard and into the kitchen.

Josh, Dink, and Ruth Rose were eating tuna sandwiches at the table. Pal was in his favorite spot, next to Josh's feet.

Four plates holding sandwiches sat on the counter. Near each plate were a napkin, a glass of milk, and two cookies.

"Where are Mom and Dad?" Bradley asked Josh.

"Dad went to get a haircut for Father's Day," Josh said. "And Mom is on a secret mission."

"Secret?" Brian said. "Cool, tell us!"

"She didn't even tell me," Josh said. "Wash your hands, please."

"They're clean," Brian said. "We just washed Polly and our hands at the same time."

Josh inspected his little brothers' hands. "Wash again now, please. Use a brush on those fingernails."

The four younger kids lined up at the sink and washed.

"What're you kids doing in the garden?" Dink asked.

The four kids took turns explaining how some creature was biting and ruining the strawberries and some of the other stuff.

"We built a scarecrow, but that didn't work," Lucy said.

"Then we dug a hole in the ground and made a trap, but nothing fell in," Nate said.

"No matter what we try, the creature is still eating strawberries," Bradley said.

"What kind of creature?" Ruth Rose asked.

"It has a big mouth," Lucy said.

"And a real long neck," Nate said.

"It's real sneaky," Brian added.

"Sounds like Josh is your creature," Dink said.

Everyone laughed.

After lunch, Bradley, Brian, Nate,

and Lucy went back to the garden.

They removed the bricks. They pulled the net off the strawberry patch.

"I don't believe it," Bradley said. He fell onto his knees.

Before lunch, at least ten strawberries had been perfect. Now five were bitten in half.

8
The Monster Is Smart, but Lucy Is Smarter

"This is creeping me out," Nate said. "No matter what we do, this . . . this . . . THING outsmarts us."

Lucy picked one of the chewed berries off the plant. "It seems like the creature waits till we're gone before he gets the berries," she said. "It could be watching us, waiting for us to leave."

"Yeah, but where is it?" Brian asked. "And how does it get inside the fence?"

"Maybe it's already inside the fence," Bradley said. He looked at the tomato plants, the zucchini plants, and the other stuff his parents had planted. "Maybe it's hiding!"

"Then we'll find it!" Brian said. "Let's check everything inside the fence."

The kids searched the garden, turning over every leaf on every plant. The only creatures they found were tiny bugs and one little toad.

"Toads are good in gardens," Lucy said. "They eat insects."

Nate held the small toad in his hand. "Could this be our monster?" he asked.

"No, his mouth is way too small," Lucy said.

"We might as well give up," Brian said.

"You can if you want," Bradley said. "But I'm not stopping till I find this berry-biting monster. I'll stay here forever if I have to!"

"Till you're old and gray?" Nate asked.

"Yep," Bradley said.

"Even when it snows in December?" Brian teased.

"Yeah, I'll build an igloo and sit in it all winter!" Bradley said, trying not to smile.

"I have an idea," Lucy said.

The three boys looked at her.

"If this creature is watching us, maybe we can play a trick on him!" she said.

"How do we do that?" Brian asked.

"We pretend to leave the garden," Lucy said. "But we don't really go away, we just hide. Maybe we'll catch him in the act!"

"But if we can see the creature, the creature can see us," Bradley said. "There's no place in this garden to hide."

"We can make something," Lucy

said. She picked up one end of the net. "In your encyclopedia you showed us those men who dug a deep hole for the buffalo. Remember the picture that showed the men hiding in some bushes and tall weeds? We can do the same thing!"

"Um, there are no tall weeds," Nate said. "We pulled them all up, remember? And we never got our ice cream, either."

"Watch," Lucy said. She grabbed some of the weeds from the pile they'd made. She wove the weed stems through the holes in the net. She added more weeds, weaving them in and out.

"I see what you're doing!" Bradley said. "It's camouflage, like army guys use when they're hiding!"

"When we're done, we can hide behind it," Lucy said. "The creature won't be able to see us."

"Awesome!" Nate said.

The four kids worked fast, weaving weeds into the net. Soon it was a thick blanket of stems and leaves.

"Drag it to the scarecrow," Lucy said. "We'll throw it over his head."

It was heavy, but they managed to hoist the camouflaged net over the scarecrow's head. The net made a sort of tent where they could crouch and hide.

The kids sat on the ground behind the net. They each poked a hole so they could peek out at the strawberry patch.

"At least this thing blocks the sun," Brian said.

"And the breeze," Nate complained. "I'm roasting."

"Just think about ice cream," Bradley said.

"That's all I've been doing," Nate said.

"We should be quiet," Lucy whispered. "The creature can probably hear us."

The kids sat silently behind the net. Flies and mosquitoes buzzed around them. A tiny bird landed on the net and pecked at a blossom. They heard an airplane fly over.

Bradley closed his eyes. He thought he might lie down and take a nap. He thought about chocolate ice cream. . . .

Suddenly Lucy grabbed his arm. "I hear something," she said.

Bradley opened his eyes. He peered

through his peephole. "Oh no!" he said. He crawled out from behind the net.

Pal was standing in the middle of the strawberry patch.

"Pal, what are you doing?" Bradley asked his dog.

Brian, Nate, and Lucy stood next to Bradley.

"Pal is our mystery creature?" Brian asked.

"Bad dog!" Bradley said.

But Pal wasn't paying attention. He was digging a hole and barking. Dirt flew up behind him as he dug.

Bradley ran over and grabbed Pal's collar. "Stop!" he said.

Pal stopped digging, but he kept barking.

Bradley looked into the hole Pal had dug. He saw a smooth rock in the bottom of the hole. Then he saw something else. The rock had four legs and a head.

9

Pal Is Pretty Smart, Too

"Guys, come and see what Pal dug up!" Bradley said.

Brian, Nate, and Lucy joined Bradley. They all peered into the hole Pal had dug.

"It's a turtle!" Nate said.

The turtle pulled its head and legs inside its shell.

Bradley lifted the turtle out of the hole. He set it on the ground.

The turtle was round on top and about eight inches long. Its shell was dark brown with bright yellow markings. Pal was quivering and whimpering.

"Where's the head?" Brian asked.

"Inside the shell," Lucy said. "This is a box turtle. Part of the stomach shell can open and close, with a hinge like on a door. It pulls its head inside to hide."

"Did it eat our strawberries?" Bradley asked.

"I think so," Lucy said. "We had one in school back home. We fed it berries all the time. They have very long necks!"

"And they live underground sometimes," Nate said. "I saw a movie about them on TV."

"Why is he hiding his head?" Brian asked.

"He's scared," Lucy said. "If we leave him alone, he'll stick his head out and start to walk."

The kids sat silently and watched the box turtle. Bradley put his arm around

Pal. After a few minutes the front of the turtle's chest shell began to open. First the nose peeked out. The shell opened more, and the head came out.

"That is so cool!" Brian whispered.

"Look what he has in his mouth," Lucy said.

The kids scooted closer to the turtle, causing it to hide its head again.

"I saw a piece of strawberry," Bradley said. "This guy is our mystery berry biter!"

"What should we do with him?" Nate asked.

"We can't leave him here!" Brian said. "He'll eat everything!"

"And if it's a mama turtle, she'll have babies and they'll eat everything, too!" Nate said.

"Box turtles like to be near wet places like bogs or swamps," Lucy said.

"Let's take it to the river," Bradley suggested.

Bradley, Brian, Nate, and Lucy left the garden. They headed across the field behind the Pintos' property. Lucy carried the box turtle. Pal trotted in front of them, sniffing the ground.

Five minutes later they came to the river. Sunlight reflected off the surface, making the water look like golden coins.

"Should we put him in the water?" Bradley asked.

"Let's let the turtle decide," Lucy said. "We'll just leave him and see where he goes."

Lucy set the turtle on the muddy riverbank. After a moment, the turtle's head and legs appeared. It slowly walked away from the water and disappeared into a pile of leaves under an oak tree.

"I hope he doesn't come back to eat more strawberries," Bradley said.

"If he does, at least we'll know

where to look for him," his brother said.

"Now you can tell your father you saved his garden!" Lucy said.

"I still want to make him strawberry jam," Bradley said. He sighed. "I guess we'll have to think of something else, though."

The kids went back to the garden. They filled in the hole they had dug for the trap. They did the same with the one Pal had dug. Just then Bradley's dad pulled into the driveway. He came over to see what they were doing.

Bradley told him about the box turtle that had been eating the strawberries. "We took him down by the river," he added.

"I'm proud of you kids," Mr. Pinto said. "You did a great job on the weeding, too. How about some ice cream?"

"Yay!" Nate yelled. "My stomach loves you, Mr. Pinto."

10
One More Job to Do

Bradley's parents and all seven kids ate ice cream on the back porch. When they were finished, Bradley's mom handed her husband a list. "Honey, would you mind picking up these things in town?" she asked.

Mr. Pinto looked at the list. "There are four different stores here," he said. "I'll bring the kids with me, and we can split up the shopping."

"No, I need the kids here!" Mrs. Pinto said. She smiled. "I have a special job for them."

"Another job!" Brian wailed. "I've been catching wild animals all day!"

Mr. Pinto got into his car and drove away.

"Okay, kids, into the kitchen!" Bradley's mother said.

"What's going on, Mom?" Bradley asked.

"You'll see," she said. "All of you follow me!"

The seven kids trooped into the kitchen. The first thing Bradley noticed was about eight baskets of strawberries on the counter. Then he saw mixing bowls, sugar, and lemons.

"What's up with this, Mom?" Josh asked.

"We're going to make strawberry jam for Daddy," his mother said, tying on an apron. "And we have to be finished by the time he gets home."

Bradley beamed. "That's why you sent him shopping!" he said.

"Yes, and when he gets to the hardware store, Mr. Carmady is going to keep him busy," his mother said. "I think we have almost two hours!"

"This is cool, Mom," Brian said.

"How did you know we wanted to make strawberry jam for Dad?" Bradley asked.

"A little bird told me," his mother said. "Actually, it was Josh. He overheard you talking about making strawberry jam. I think it's a wonderful present, and Dad will love knowing we made it from his mother's recipe. I bought the strawberries from Perry's Farm this morning."

Bradley's mother had Grandma Pinto's jam recipe in her hand. "Now each of us will have a job," she said. "If we work together, we'll be done before Dad gets back."

She handed the recipe card to Lucy. "Lucy, your job is to read us the recipe. Make sure we follow all of Grandma Pinto's instructions. Okay, now let's get busy!"

• • •

The next morning when Bradley and Brian came down to the kitchen, their father was sitting at the table. He was getting ready to spread butter on his toast.

"Wait a second, Dad," Bradley said. He ran out of the room, then came back with Josh and their mom. They each placed a small jar on the table. Every jar had a label that read:

"HAPPY FATHER'S DAY!" they all yelled.

"Where did this come from?" their father asked. He had a big grin on his face.

"We made it," Brian said. "We all helped, but it was Bradley's idea."

Bradley's father twisted the lid off one of the jars. He picked up a spoon and dipped it in. He put a lump of jam in his mouth.

Everyone else stood and watched.

Bradley had his fingers crossed.

Mr. Pinto closed his eyes as he tasted the jam.

Then he opened his eyes. Bradley thought he saw tears.

"Is it as good as your mom's jam?" Josh asked.

His father grinned. "It's perfect," he said. "This is the best present ever!"

How many of KC and Marshall's adventures have you read?

Capital Mysteries

1. WHO CLONED THE PRESIDENT?
by Ron Roy

2. KIDNAPPED AT THE CAPITAL
by Ron Roy

3. THE SKELETON IN THE SMITHSONIAN
by Ron Roy

4. A SPY IN THE WHITE HOUSE
by Ron Roy

5. WHO BROKE LINCOLN'S THUMB?
by Ron Roy

6. FIREWORKS AT THE FBI
by Ron Roy

7. TROUBLE AT THE TREASURY
by Ron Roy

8. MYSTERY AT THE WASHINGTON MONUMENT
by Ron Roy

9. A THIEF AT THE NATIONAL ZOO
by Ron Roy

10. THE ELECTION-DAY DISASTER
by Ron Roy

11. THE SECRET AT JEFFERSON'S MANSION
by Ron Roy

12. THE GHOST AT CAMP DAVID
by Ron Roy

13. TRAPPED ON THE D.C. TRAIN!
by Ron Roy

If you like Calendar Mysteries, you might want to read A to Z Mysteries!

Help Dink, Josh, and Ruth Rose . . .

. . . solve mysteries from A to Z!